James Stevenson

UN-HAPPY NEW YEAR, EMMA!

Greenwillow Books
New York

Library of Congress Cataloging-in-Publication Data
Stevenson, James (date)
Un-Happy New Year, Emma! / by James Stevenson.
p.   cm.
Summary: Emma struggles in her New Year's resolution to
be nicer to the other witches Dolores and Lavinia, as they
persist in being dreadful to her, until their relationship
climaxes in a dreadful revenge on New Year's Day.
ISBN 0-688-08342-0.   ISBN 0-688-08343-9 (lib. bdg.)
[1. Witches—Fiction.   2. New Year—Fiction.
3. Cartoons and comics.]   I. Title.
II. Title: Unhappy New Year, Emma!   PZ7.S84748Un 1989
[E]—dc19   88-18802   CIP   AC

FOOF!

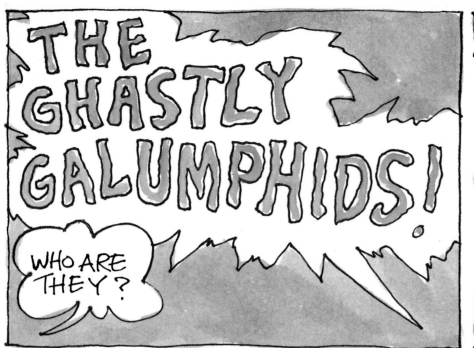